© Disney·Pixar
© Disney
D1309260

Rapunzel's hair is long and strong!

Rapunzel wants to go see the floating lights up close.

Mother Gothel tells Rapunzel she is not allowed to leave the tower.

It is almost Rapunzel's eighteenth birthday.

Flynn Rider is on the run from the palace guards.

Maximus is a palace horse. His job is to find Flynn.

Flynn needs a place to hide!

Flynn climbs up Rapunzel's secret tower.

Rapunzel bops Flynn on the head with a frying pan.

Rapunzel finds a crown in Flynn's satchel.

Rapunzel is surprised that the crown fits.
Look at the top picture carefully. Then circle three
things that are different in the bottom picture.

ANSWER:

Flynn agrees to take Rapunzel to see the floating lights.

Rapunzel finally feels free!

Mother Gothel knows that Rapunzel has left the tower!

Flynn brings Rapunzel to the Snuggly Duckling.

Maximus and the royal guard have come to the Snuggly Duckling to capture Flynn.

Flynn and Rapunzel are shown a way to escape.

Flynn and Rapunzel walk through a long tunnel.

Rapunzel's magical hair heals a cut on Flynn's hand.

Maximus finds Flynn! Rapunzel holds on tight!

Since it is Rapunzel's birthday,
Maximus and Flynn agree to work together.

Rapunzel is amazed when she sees the kingdom!

Draw a line from each picture to its close-up.

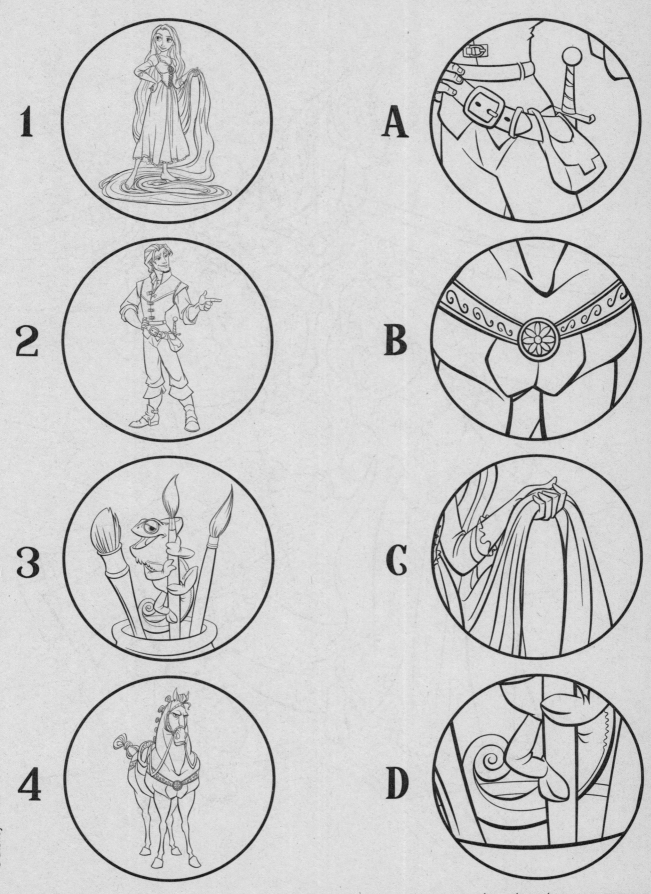

1

2

3

4

A

B

C

D

ANSWER: 1-C, 2-A, 3-D, and 4-B.

Rapunzel crosses the bridge to enter the kingdom.

Rapunzel is having the best day ever!

Rapunzel's dream has come true—she sees the floating lights!

Flynn and Rapunzel launch a floating lantern together.

Rapunzel gives Flynn his satchel.

Rapunzel is sad to see Flynn sail away.

Flynn is in the royal jail.

Rapunzel tells Mother Gothel that she knows the truth.
To find out who Rapunzel really is, begin at the *T* and write
the letters in order on the blanks.

___ ____   ➡ T H E
L O S
_____   T P R
I N C
E S S

© Disney

Maximus brings Flynn to rescue Rapunzel.

At last, Rapunzel is back home with her mother and father.

Flynn is happy to give the crown to its true owner.

THE PRINCESS
AND THE
FROG

Tiana lives in New Orleans. She loves to cook with her father.

Tiana shares gumbo with her neighbors.

© Disney

Tiana grows up and works hard.

Tiana is as pretty as a fairy-tale princess.
Look up, down, forward, backward, and diagonally to see
how many times you can find the name TIANA in the puzzle.

A T I A N A
A T A N I T
N A I T N I
A I T A A A
I N I T N N
T I A N A A
N A N I I T
A N A I T N

ANSWER: 9.

© Disney

Tiana makes a wish on the Evening Star.

Prince Naveen surprises Tiana. A spell turned him into a frog!

Naveen asks for a kiss. He hopes it will make him human again.

Now Tiana is a frog, too!

Tiana and Naveen hold on tight and float away.

Uh-oh! The alligators look hungry!

Louis is a friendly alligator.

Louis knows someone who can turn Tiana and Naveen human again.

Tiana gives Naveen cooking lessons.

Everyone loves Tiana's special gumbo.

Naveen helps Tiana dance and have fun.

Mama Odie can help Tiana and Naveen.

Naveen has a gift for Tiana.

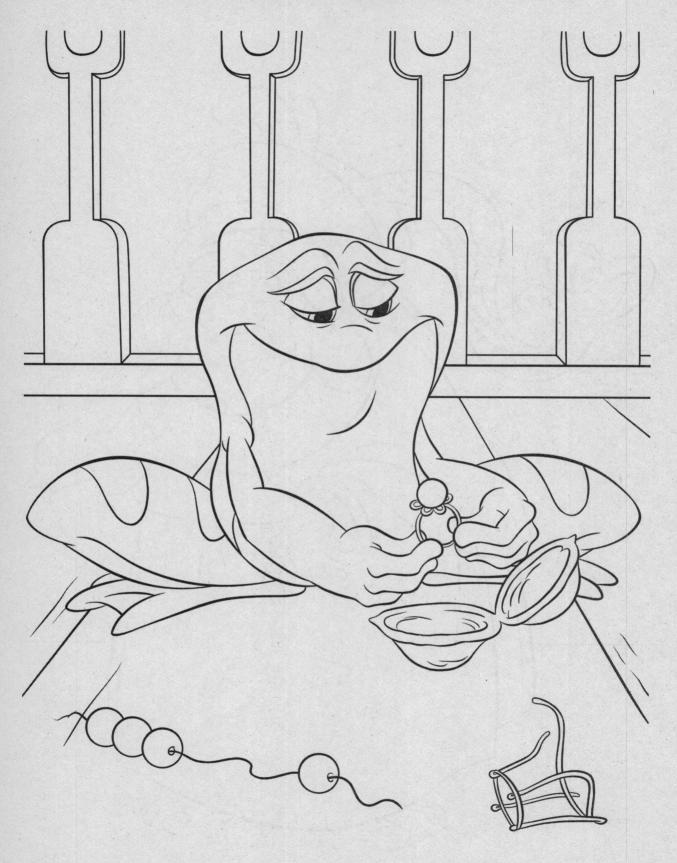

Tiana and Naveen have fallen in love.

Tiana is upset when she thinks Charlotte is going to marry Naveen.

Charlotte learns that her prince is a fake.

Tiana and Naveen want to spend their lives together—even if they remain frogs.

Mama Odie marries Tiana and Naveen.

True love is magical!

Prince Naveen kisses his new princess—and the spell is broken!

Draw a line between each picture and its close-up.

Princess Tiana is a beautiful bride.

Tiana and Naveen have a royal wedding, too.

Tiana finally has her restaurant.

Tiana and Naveen know that dreams do come true!

Ariel is a little mermaid who loves to sing.

Ariel swims around with her friends Flounder and Sebastian.

Sebastian is a crab.

Ariel and Sebastian are ready to celebrate.

Ariel makes a wish upon a star.

Ariel greets her undersea friends.

Flounder helps Ariel check out a new hairstyle.

Which line will lead Ariel to Flounder?

Ariel likes to collect treasures from the human world.

Ariel's favorite treasure is her statue of Prince Eric.

Sweet dreams!

Ariel daydreams about Prince Eric.

Connect the dots to see what Ariel and Flounder have found.

Look at all the treasures!

Scuttle gives Ariel a gift.

Scuttle uses the dinglehopper to give himself an interesting hairstyle!

Ariel and Flounder swim to a nearby ship.

Prince Eric doesn't know Ariel and Scuttle are watching him.

Ariel is in love!

Ariel's dream has come true—she's a human!

Prince Eric's dog, Max, discovers Ariel on the beach.

Eric and Ariel enjoy a boat ride.

It's Ariel's wedding day!

Ariel is excited to marry Prince Eric.

Ariel's friends and family are at the ceremony.

Sebastian sings as the happy couple dances.

Ariel's sisters hope to catch the bouquet.

Time to cut the wedding cake!

King Triton hugs his daughter.

Ariel thanks everyone for coming to her wedding.

Eric gives Ariel a horse named Beau.

Ariel brushes Beau's soft coat.

Beau gets a tasty treat.

Scuttle comes to meet Beau.

Ariel shows Scuttle her beautiful new necklace.

Ariel and Eric dance in the moonlight.

The mice are always happy to help Cinderella.

The mice and birds have made a beautiful dress for Cinderella.

The Fairy Godmother gets Cinderella ready for the royal ball.

Cinderella curtsies when she meets the Prince.

The Prince asks Cinderella to dance.

Cinderella and the Prince fall in love as they dance.

Cinderella is excited for her wedding day.

Everyone is happy for the royal couple.

The Prince and Cinderella dance for the first time
as husband and wife.

© Disney

Cinderella and her Prince ride off in their wedding carriage.

Cinderella likes visiting the royal stables.

Cinderella's horse is named Frou.

Frou loves to munch on apples.

Cinderella takes an exciting ride!

Cinderella and the Prince enjoy breakfast outside.

Cinderella tries to write in her diary every day.

Cinderella joins her friends in the royal garden.

Jaq and Gus help the princess pick flowers.

The flowers look perfect!

The Prince is heading out for a ride.

Cinderella and the Prince enjoy a dance in the moonlight.

Angus is a powerful Clydesdale.

Merida's father is a strong warrior king.

Queen Elinor is Merida's mother.

Merida has three brothers.
Circle the picture that is different from the others.

1

2

3

4

5

Merida's parents teach her how to tame falcons.

Merida doesn't like her music lessons.

Sword-fighting with King Fergus is lots of fun!

Merida is a good climber!

Spending time with Angus is Merida's favorite thing to do.

Merida is upset to learn she must get married.

Queen Elinor tries to tell Merida that it is important to follow tradition.

Merida is getting ready to meet the lords and their sons.

Merida doesn't like anything about this traditional dress!

The Highland Games are about to begin.

Bagpipes play as the lords enter the castle.

An archery contest will decide who gets to marry Merida.

Merida decides to compete in the contest, too.

Merida has the best shot!

Merida cuts her family tapestry.

Merida and Angus ride deep into the forest.

Merida discovers a witch's cottage in the woods.

The witch prepares a spell cake for Merida.

Merida serves the spell cake to her mother.

© Disney•Pixar

Queen Elinor turns into a bear!

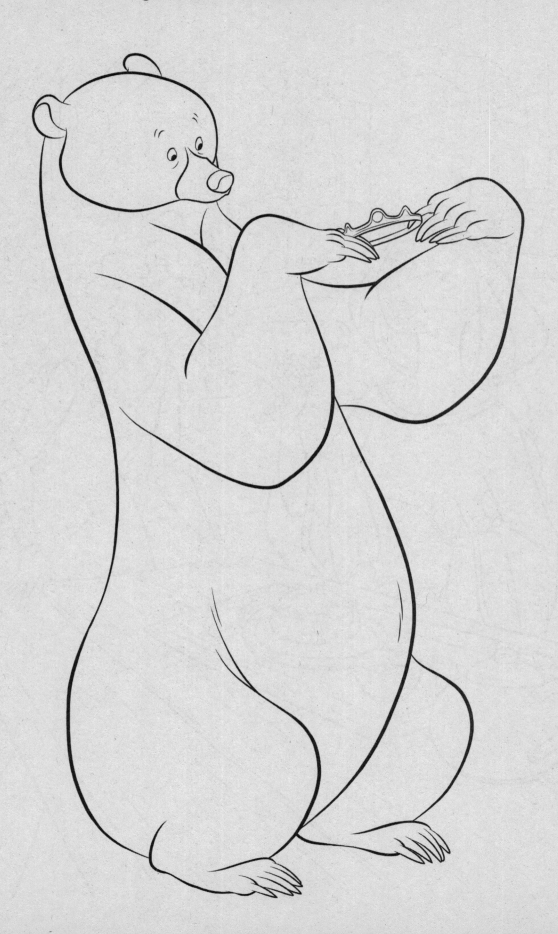

Oh, no! Merida's brothers want some cake, too.

Merida and her mother can't find the witch's cottage.

Merida helps her mother catch fish.

Merida wants her mother to be human again.

Merida thinks she knows how to break the spell.

Merida's brothers are now cute bear cubs!

Follow the lines to find out the names of the identical cubs.

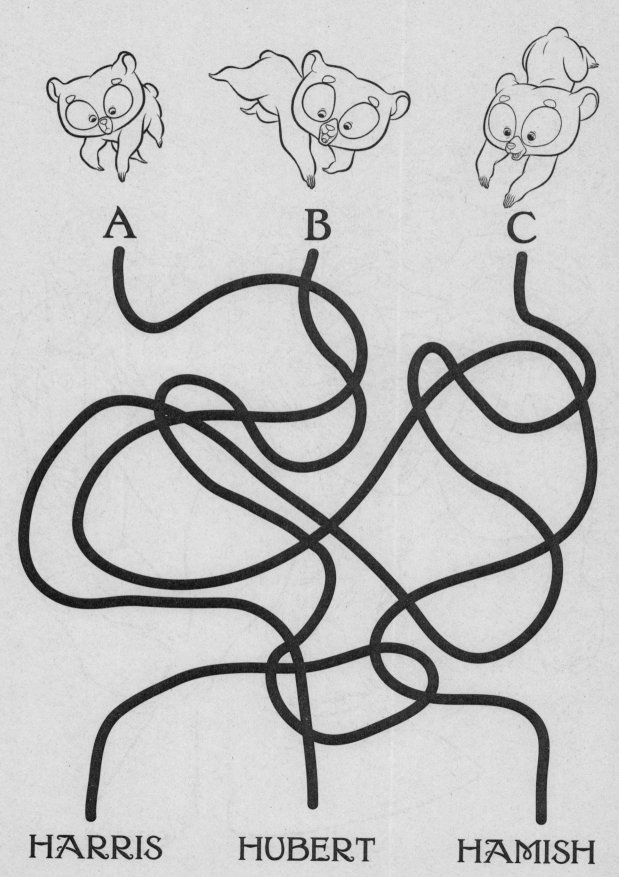

A   B   C

HARRIS   HUBERT   HAMISH

ANSWER: A-Hamish, B-Harris, C-Hubert.

Merida tries to repair the tapestry as she rides back to her mother.

Fixing the tapestry did not break the spell. Merida tells her mother she loves her—even if she is a bear.

Queen Elinor is human again!

The boys are human again, too!

Merida and her mother decide to make a new tapestry.

Queen Elinor and her brave daughter now go on adventures together.

Aurora dances and laughs with her animal friends.

The animals love hearing Aurora's stories.

The squirrels look forward to Aurora's visits.

Aurora whistles and the birds sing back.

Aurora spots a nest of baby birds.

Aurora shares her berries.

Fauna, Flora, and Merryweather take care of Aurora.

A bunny helps pick flowers with Aurora.

Aurora gives the pretty flowers to Flora.

Aurora takes a walk in the forest.

Aurora and Prince Phillip meet in the forest.

The animals watch as Phillip and Aurora dance.

The prince plays a lovely song for Aurora.

"Watch your step!"

Teatime with friends is always nice.

Phillip loves to hear Aurora sing.

Prince Phillip gives Aurora a lovely bouquet.

Today is Aurora's wedding day!

Any day with the good fairies is a magical day!

Aurora's friends get her ready for the wedding.

Phillip and Aurora are married outdoors.

Phillip and Aurora are a beautiful couple.

What a perfect day!

Circle the dress that matches the one Aurora is wearing.

Aurora loves it when the good fairies visit her at the palace.

The good fairies admire Aurora's new crown.

Prince Phillip and Princess Aurora are very happy.

Aurora walks past the castle fountain.

The royal garden is one of Aurora's favorite places.

© Disney

Aurora tries on a new dress.

Aurora and Phillip dance in the castle.

The word *crown* starts with the letter C.
Find and circle three other items that begin with C.

Prince Phillip takes Aurora to the royal stables.

Aurora gives Buttercup a hug.